MATT AND DAVE

YUCK

YUCK'S BIG
BOGEYS
AND
YUCK'S SMELLY
SOCKS

Illustrated by Nigel Baines

www.yuckweb.com

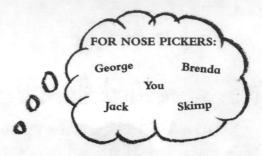

FOR NOSE PICKERS:

George   Brenda
You
Jack   Skimp

SIMON AND SCHUSTER

First published in Great Britain in 2006
by Simon & Schuster UK Ltd
A CBS COMPANY

Africa House 64–78 Kingsway London WC2B 6AH

5 7 9 10 8 6 4

A CIP catalogue record for this book is
available from the British Library

ISBN-13: 978-1-4169-1093-0

Typeset by Nigel Baines
Printed and bound in Great Britain by
Cox & Wyman Ltd Reading Berkshire

www.simonsays.co.uk

There was a boy so disgusting they called him Yuck

YUCK'S BIG BOGEYS

"Stop picking," Mum said.

"I wasn't."

Mum looked round from the front seat of the car.

"Yes you were. I saw you."

"I wasn't doing anything," Yuck said.

Polly Princess was sitting next to him.

"You're disgusting, Yuck," she said.

Dad was driving. Polly reached over and tapped him on the shoulder.

Dad glanced in his mirror. "Yuck, stop picking your nose!"

Yuck wiped his finger on the car seat.

Just one more pick and...

"Use a tissue!" Mum told him.

"But Mum..."

Mum opened her handbag and
rummaged for a tissue.

Yuck had just enough time to slip his finger up his nose.

Nearly got it. Just a little bit...

The bogey was on the end of his finger.

PICTURE
TAKEN
WITH
SNOT
CAM

PLOP! The bogey was in his mouth.

"Yuck! That's revolting!" Polly said. She turned away and looked out of the car window.

Nice, Yuck thought, rolling the bogey with his tongue.

"You are absolutely the most repulsive brother ever," Polly muttered.

Chewy, Yuck thought, pressing the bogey between his teeth.

"Dad, did you see what Yuck just did?"

But Dad was busy driving.

Mum reached round from the front seat with a tissue in her hand. She pinched it over Yuck's nose.

"Blow," she said.

Yuck groaned.

"Yuck, do as your mum tells you," Dad said, turning the corner into their street.

Yuck huffed once into the tissue.

"Blow properly," Mum said.

Yuck huffed again.

"It's not fair," he complained, as they pulled up at the house. "Why can't I pick my nose?"

"Because I said so," Mum told him.

Yuck decided that when he was EMPEROR OF EVERYTHING, everyone would have to pick their nose – it would be THE LAW. He'd collect all the bogeys in a great big bogey pit, and anyone found with a tissue would be dunked into it head first on a big bogey bungee jump.

Mum opened the car door and marched Yuck to the house.

At home that evening, she kept a close eye on him.

She caught him picking his nose behind the sofa.

She caught him picking his nose in the treehouse.

She caught him picking his nose in the cupboard under the stairs.

And when it was time for bed, she burst in on Yuck in his bedroom. He was hiding under the covers in the middle of an experiment, trying to get two fingers up one nostril. They were halfway up and about to pull out a long stringy bogey.

MORE SNOTCAM INSIDE YUCK'S NOSE

"Don't you dare!" Mum said, lifting his duvet.

Yuck groaned and pulled his fingers out slowly, trying not to snap the bogey as it stretched. It pinged loose from his nostril. But just as he was about to eat it, Mum wiped his hand with a tissue.

"Skids!" Yuck swore. He'd been growing the bogey for an hour.

"Put these on!" Mum said.

She handed him a pair of red mittens.

"But I'm not cold," Yuck told her.

"They're not for the cold. They're for nose pickers."

Yuck put the red mittens on. His fingers were trapped.

"They're itchy," he complained.

"They're to stop you picking your nose."

Mum put a box of tissues by the side of Yuck's bed and went back downstairs.

But the red mittens were no match for Yuck...

That night, he dreamed he was inside a nose as big as a cave. It was full of huge green bogey boulders. He pushed one and rolled it away, and from underneath it two red snakes appeared. They coiled themselves around his hands. He pushed and fought, wrestling the snakes to the ground and rolling the bogey boulder to the front of the cave.

In the morning he woke up sneezing. His nostrils were stuffed full with red wool. His fingernails were covered in woolly bogeys. He'd picked his way right through the mittens!

Yuck wiggled his fingers.

"Rockits! What a pick!"

He hopped out of bed, threw on his clothes and went downstairs for breakfast.

"What happened to your mittens?" Mum asked. She grabbed his hands and inspected them.

"It wasn't me," Yuck said. "It was moths – mitten-eating moths. They attacked in the night. They must have flown in through the window."

"You've ruined a perfectly good pair
of mittens, Yuck!"

"Honest, Mum. It wasn't me. I've stopped
picking my nose."

"He's lying!" Polly said.

"Really, Mum. From now on I'm using
tissues."

Dad looked at Yuck and scratched his head. "What did you say, Yuck?"

"I'm never going to pick my nose again, Dad," Yuck promised.

"Don't believe him!" Polly said. "He's lying! Once a nose picker, always a nose picker."

"Not me," Yuck said.

From his pocket he pulled out a tissue and blew his nose on it.

"Well I never," Mum said.

"It's a miracle," Dad said.

"He's up to something," Polly whispered.

Yuck pulled a face at Polly and, as she went to eat a mouthful of muesli, he showed her the contents of his tissue.

"Go away! You're gross," Polly told him.

"It's OK, Polly, I know you're just jealous."

"Jealous? Why would I be jealous of you?"

"Because you want to share my reward."

"Reward?"

Polly looked at Mum.

Yuck quickly shook his tissue over Polly's bowl of muesli.

"That's right," Yuck said, sitting down in his seat. "My reward for not picking my nose for a whole week."

"And what's that, Yuck?" Mum asked.

"Sweets!"

Yuck looked at Mum hopefully.

Mum looked at Dad.

"A whole week?" Dad said. "That's impossible."

"OK, Yuck, one whole week of not picking your nose and you can have a jumbo scoop of sweets from Candy Joe's," Mum said.

"Rockits!" Yuck said, pouring himself a bowl of Monster Snaps.

"But one pick and the deal's off," Dad told him.

"And what about me?" Polly moaned. "I don't ever pick my nose but I don't get a reward."

"You can have a scoop too, darling," Mum told her.

"Good. Then I'll get lots of sweets and Yuck will get none because he'll NEVER manage to stop picking his nose!"

Yuck giggled. His nose twitched, and the Nose-Pick Challenge began...

On Saturday morning, Yuck watched *GROSSOUT!* on television. In the afternoon, he counted his scabs, and in the evening he won three extra lives on *SKID WARS*. All day his nose tingled, but he didn't pick it – just as he'd promised.

What no one knew was that he didn't blow it either. Yuck was a Bogeyman with a Bogeyplan – he was going to grow the world's biggest bogeys! He'd get his sweets and he'd get his revenge too – SWEET REVENGE!

All day the snot built in Yuck's nose, and that night his bogeys began to grow. He dreamed he was in BOGEYLAND. He wore bogey shorts and bogey shoes, and snot instead of socks. He drove a bogey car

over bogey roads and lived in a bogey
house. He had bogey chairs and a bogey
bed and even a bogey cat.

And everything was pickable!

By Sunday morning, a whole night's worth of gunk had collected in Yuck's nose. As the gunk dried, it turned crusty and began to itch. His Bogeyplan was hatching.

All morning Polly Princess spied on him, desperate to catch him picking.

When everyone sat at the table to eat their Sunday lunch, Yuck noticed her watching him. He waited until Polly was looking, then pinched a pea between his fingers and slipped it into his mouth.

"Mum, Yuck just ate a bogey. _____
him!" Polly said.

"No I didn't!"

Yuck opened his mouth for Mum
to inspect.

"It's a pea," Mum said.

Yuck stuck his tongue out at Polly.
"Serves you right for spying on me," he
told her. And he grinned and went upstairs
to his room.

That afternoon, Yuck busied himself
by drawing a Bogey Chart. In bright green
pen, he wrote the days, 1 to 7, down the
side of a piece of paper.

Next to day 1 he wrote TINGLY.

Next to day 2 he wrote ITCHY.

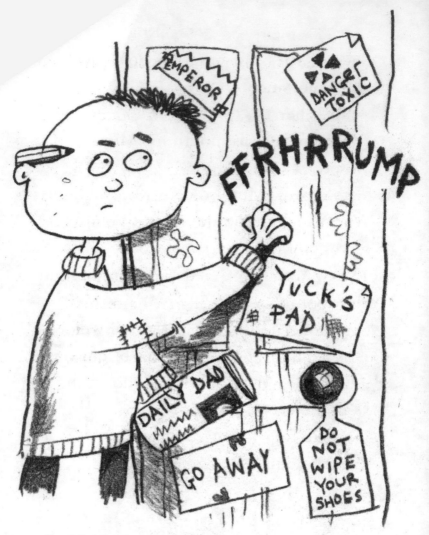

Suddenly he heard a knock.

"Is everything all right in there? Are you being good?" Dad asked from outside Yuck's door.

"I'm just blowing my nose," Yuck called.

He pretended to blow into a tissue, making a loud raspberry so Dad could hear.

"Only five days to go until Candy Joe's," Dad said.

Five days seemed a long time. But at least tomorrow, at school, there would be no one spying on him. At least that's what Yuck thought.

But on Monday, everywhere he went, Polly went too. Every corner he turned, there she was, spying on him in corridors, spying on him in the playground, spying on him in the canteen.

Juicy Lucy and Madison Snake were
helping her. They giggled each time
Yuck passed.

"Bogeyboy," they whispered.

Yuck wanted to pick his nose and
rub his bogeys into their hair, but he
stopped himself.

He had to stick to his plan. He didn't
pick and he didn't blow. And his bogeys
kept on growing!

"Well, Polly?" Mum asked, when Polly
and Yuck got home from school.

"Nothing," Polly said, disappointed.

"Hold out your hands," Mum said
to Yuck.

Mum checked under his fingernails
for bogeys.

"Well I never. They're clean. I wouldn't
have believed it if I hadn't seen it with my
own eyes. That's three whole days without
picking," Mum said.

Yuck stomped up to his room and gave
his nose a scratch. He was desperate to pick
it. It was filling up like he had a cold. With
his green pen, next to day 3 on his Bogey
Chart he wrote GOOEY.

GOOEY.

By Tuesday, there was so much snot inside his nose that it was bubbling from his nostrils, pushing its way out like toothpaste from a tube. Mum tried to grab him and wipe it, but Yuck ran into the bathroom and sniffed the snot back in, then blew a raspberry into his tissue.

"All clean now," he lied.

And all day at school the spies were watching him as he sniffed.

He chewed his fingernails.

He had a lick of earwax.

But he never picked his nose. He was determined to win.

And by the time he got home, his nostrils were so full that he had to plug them with plasticine to stop the gunk from leaking out.

Next to day 4 on his Bogey Chart he wrote GUNKY.

By Wednesday, day 5, his Bogeyplan was taking shape. At the back of his nostrils Yuck could feel two lumps — two magnificent bogeys growing in size.

He almost lost one of them playing football.

Frank the Tank was in goal. As Yuck shot to score, a bogey the size of a Brussels sprout dropped from one nostril. It hung on a string of snot a metre long.

SNOT MOTION REPLAY

Just as the string of snot was about to snap, Yuck gave an almighty sniff. The bogey shot back up his nose like a yo-yo.

"Goal!" Little Eric shouted.

Next to day 5 on his Bogey Chart Yuck wrote STRINGY.

*·STRINGY·:

His plan was working.

By Thursday, his bogeys were massive. He looked in the mirror. His nose was bulging on both sides, as if he'd stuffed socks up it.

"What's the matter with you?" Mum called to him as he ran out of the house.

"Bees. I got stung by nose-stinging bees," Yuck told her. "They must have flown in the window with the mitten-eating moths."

And all day at school he could hardly breathe through his nose, and his voice sounded funny when he spoke.

Polly and her spies teased him.

"Sore nose, Yuck? Dat's derrible. Why don'd you pick id?"

But Yuck didn't. He wanted his bogeys to grow even bigger.

Next to day 6 on his Bogey Chart
he wrote LUMPY.

Only one more day and SWEET
REVENGE would be his!

That night, Yuck dreamed he met
Candy Joe.

The sweets supremo was wearing black
liquorice shoes tied with strawberry laces
and a fudge cap on his head. Candy Joe
gave Yuck a jelly snake that wriggled in his
hand. Fizzing saucers whizzed past Yuck's
ears and chocolate bombs exploded all
around him. He sledged, mouth first, down
a mountain of sherbet, and splash-landed
into a sea of caramel...

It was SWEET-TASTIC.

Yuck woke with a smile and looked at his Bogey Chart.

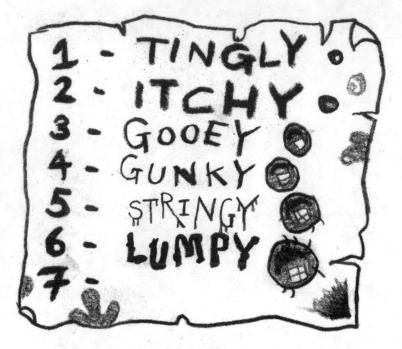

1 - TINGLY
2 - ITCHY
3 - GOOEY
4 - GUNKY
5 - STRINGY
6 - LUMPY
7 -

He knew exactly what he wanted to write next to day 7…

BOGEY!

IT WAS…

Just a few hours stood between him and
SWEET REVENGE!

All day at school, Yuck stayed undercover.

He sat at the back in every lesson, hiding
his nose in his hands. At lunchtime he hid
in the boys' toilets with his head under the
cold tap to stop his nose exploding.

His bogeys were massive – the world's
biggest bogeys!

When the bell rang and school was
finally over, Mum came to collect him
and Polly.

"Well, have you been good, Yuck?"

"I dink so," Yuck said, his nose swollen to the size of his fist.

"Anything to report, Polly?" Mum asked.

"Nothing," Polly replied, scowling. She hadn't caught Yuck picking all week.

Yuck held out his hands. Mum checked his nails.

"Well I never — absolutely bogey free!" she said. "It looks like we're going to Candy Joe's after all."

"Roggits!" Yuck said.

Candy Joe's was the best sweet shop ever!
Yuck chose white chocolate splats and
caramel bursts, toffee tongue-twisters and
lemonade licks. He ummed and ahhed
about which were best – shiny chocolate
coins or sugar-dusted strawberry suckers.

He paused over pear drops and puzzled over the butterscotch balls, dribbled over the peanut spirals and went loopy over the treacle whirls. He had one each of anything jelly and six of Candy Joe's special SWEET OF THE WEEK.

Driving back from Candy Joe's, he sat in the back of the car with chocolate round his mouth, and with his jumbo scoop of sweets poured out across his lap.

Polly sat in the front seat next to Mum.

"Thank you, Mum," Polly said, picking a pink cherry heart from her scoop.

"Danks, Bum," Yuck said, scoffing a handful of fizzbees.

"You both earned it," Mum said. "I must admit, I never thought you'd be able to do it, Yuck."

"I dold you, Bum. I don'd bick by dose any bore. I use dissues," Yuck said.

He sucked on a triple-dipped chocolate finger, planning his revenge.

"Ooobbs, I've just drobbed by dissue," he said, ducking down behind Mum's seat.

It was time for the final part of his Bogeyplan.

Yuck sniffed and snorted.

Out of sight of Polly and Mum, he had the biggest pick ever.

First he used one finger and then two.
Then he used the stick of his loadsalollipop
and then the spoon from his sherbert dunk.

Gradually he worked one sticky lump
from the back of his nose to the front.

A huge bogey burst out.

It throbbed in the palm of his hand.

It was enormous – a superbogey – the biggest, snottiest, stickiest bogey that Yuck had ever seen. It was as big as a golfball.

Yuck bent down again, pretending to blow into his tissue. He pressed one nostril closed and blasted the other.

A second bogey shot out like a cannonball and splatted against the back of Mum's seat. Yuck scooped it off.

It was magnificent – just as big, just as snotty and just as sticky as the first.

Yuck rolled the bogeys in his hands, round and round, until each one was shiny and smooth. All week he had been waiting for this moment.

He grinned.

"This is such a fantastic jumbo scoop of

sweets," he said, sitting back up in his seat. "Especially the gobstoppers – they're the best!"

"Gobstoppers?" Polly Princess said. "I didn't see any gobstoppers at Candy Joe's."

"They were in a jar at the back," Yuck said. "SUPERSTOPPERS. The biggest and best gobstoppers in the world."

"SUPERSTOPPERS! That's not fair. I didn't get any. Can we go back, Mum?" Polly asked.

"Oh Polly, we're nearly home now."

"Please, Mum," Polly whined.

"Don't worry, you can share mine," Yuck told her.

"That's very kind of you, Yuck," Mum said. "How nice of you to think about your sister. Say thank you, Polly."

"Thank you," Polly mumbled.

"Would you like one, too, Mum? They're ever so tasty," Yuck said.

"I'd love one, Yuck, thank you. It's been years since I had a gobstopper."

Yuck handed Polly and Mum one each –
the two big green ones in his hands.

"They're huge!" Polly said.

"They're a lot stickier than I remember," Mum said.

"That's because they're SUPERSTOPPERS – the biggest and best in the world," Yuck said.

Mum opened her mouth and popped hers in.

She sucked.

"Mmm, tasty."
"Mine's delicious,"
Polly said, struggling
to chew, as if her
mouth was full
of glue.

Yuck giggled.

"That's because they're homemade."

YUCK'S SMELLY SOCKS

Yuck opened his sock drawer – long socks, short socks, school socks, sports socks and socks with holes. Socks of all different colours – some with stripes and some with spots. Some were in pairs and some were not. But every sock was CLEAN!

"Skids!" Yuck swore. "What's the point of clean socks?"

He closed the drawer and opened the lid of the glass tank at the end of his bed – his smells collection. The tank belched a cloud of gas.

He fished out a pair of smelly red socks and quickly shut the lid.

The glass tank rattled.

He pressed the smelly red socks against his nose and sniffed.

"Mmmmm... dirty, crusty, cheesy socks!"

He put them on.

Yuck decided that when he was EMPEROR OF EVERYTHING, all his socks would be smelly. He would be the

King of Foot Cheese and Toe Jam.
And everyone would come from miles
around to smell his feet. It would be
the LAW!

"Have you got clean socks on today,
Yuck?" Mum asked, poking her nose
around his bedroom door.

"Yes, Mum," Yuck said.

Quickly he ran past Mum and down the stairs to the front door.

Polly Princess was waiting for him. "Hurry up, I don't want to be late for school," she said. "Miss Fortune gives me stars for being on time."

"That's because you're a goody-goody," Yuck told her.

Yuck's teacher, Mrs Wagon the Dragon, never gave him any stars.

Yuck picked up his bag and left with his sister, his socks wafting cheesy smells as he walked.

At the front of the classroom the Dragon was waving her umbrella.

"This week you are each going to write a poem," she said to the class.

Everyone groaned.

The Dragon checked that the tip of her umbrella was nice and sharp. "And at the end of the week you're going to read them out in front of the headmaster and the rest of the school."

"Do we have to, Miss?" Little Eric asked.

"Yes," the Dragon said.

She picked up a book from her desk.

"Here is the start of a famous poem by William Wordsworth," she said.

She began to read, "'I wandered lonely as a...'"

The Dragon pointed her umbrella at Schoolie Julie.

"What comes next?" she asked.

"Cheese!" Schoolie Julie said.

The class giggled.

"I wandered lonely as a cheese?"
The Dragon poked Schoolie Julie with
the point of her umbrella. "Don't be
ridiculous!" she said.

She swung the umbrella towards Megan
the Mouth. "You!" she said. "I wandered
lonely as a…"

Megan the Mouth covered her nose with
her hand.

"Cheese!" she said.

The Dragon gave Megan the Mouth a poke, then pointed her umbrella at Little Eric.

"Cheese?" Little Eric said, looking up.

The Dragon paused. Her nose twitched.

"Cheese!" she said. "I can smell CHEESE!"

"So can I!" Schoolie Julie said.

"So can I!" Megan the Mouth said.

"So can I!" the whole class said.

Everyone's noses were twitching.

The stench of strong, sweaty, smelly CHEESE was wafting from the back of the room.

Yuck was staring out of the classroom
window. His shoes were on the floor. His
feet were up on his desk and his toes were
wiggling in his smelly red socks.

"PHWOOOAAARRR!"

The class stared at him, sniffing.

"Yuck! Your socks stink!" the Dragon
bellowed.

She marched over to him, holding her
pointy nose with her fingers.

"Your socks smell of CHEESE!"

She gave Yuck a sharp poke with
her umbrella.

"Get those socks out of my classroom
this instant!" she said.

The Dragon picked Yuck up by his ear
and marched him to the door.

"But they're my favourite socks, Miss," he
said.

The Dragon handed Yuck a pencil
and paper, and pushed him out of
the classroom.

"No one wears smelly socks in my class!
You can write your poem out there!" she
said.

She made Yuck stand in the corridor,
where no one could smell him.

"And it had better be good!"

The Dragon slammed the classroom
door shut.

Yuck pressed his nose against the glass
and watched. Everyone picked up their
pencils and paper and started writing.

Yuck looked at the blank piece of paper

in his hand. He picked his ear with his
pencil. He couldn't think what to write.

I wandered lonely as a...

Poetry's boring, he thought. Smelly socks
are much more fun!

Yuck had an idea, and he skidded
off down the corridor and outside to
the dustbins.

Mrs Wagon the Dragon was going to
be in for a surprise. He was going to make
the dirtiest, crustiest, smelliest socks in the
whole wide world!

He lifted a dustbin lid and rummaged
inside.

"Rockits!" He pulled out a mouldy ham sandwich and half a banana.

Yuck stuffed the mouldy sandwich into one sock and mushed the banana into the other, then squelched back inside.

He opened the door of Mr Sweep the caretaker's store cupboard.

He looked along the shelves.

Floor polish? Oil? Soap? Grease?

Yuck took down the can of oil and the pot of grease. He squirted a long dribble of

oil into one sock and dolloped a big scoop
of grease into the other.

Then he skidded down the corridor and
stood back outside the classroom, wiggling
his toes until the end of the day.

That evening, in his bedroom, Yuck swept
the dandruff and plastic spiders off his desk,
turned his lamp on and assembled his
equipment – a spoon, his swimming
goggles and a baseball bat.

When everyone had gone to bed, he
crept to the kitchen, opened the fridge, took
out a block of cheese and tiptoed back to
his room.

Opening the lid of his smells collection, he grabbed his can of fart spray and sprayed some in his socks. Then he took out a rotten egg and placed it on his desk.

Swimming goggles on, he picked up his baseball bat and...

Yuck bashed the egg and the block of
cheese until they were sloppy and mushy.
He spooned them into his socks.

They felt squishy and gooey and lovely!
It was time to let it all stew.

He hopped into bed and wiggled his
toes, feeling everything mixing together –
the mouldy ham sandwich, the mushy
banana, the oil, the grease, the fart spray,
the rotten egg and the cheese.

With every wiggle his socks became more and more dirty and smelly.

That night, Yuck dreamed he was in a factory with cheese going past on a long conveyor belt. He was Chief Hole-Maker and he lay there dipping his toes into each block of cheese that went past.

The next morning, Yuck woke up and
sniffed. Phwoarrr!

"Have you got clean socks on?" Mum
asked him.

"Yes, Mum," Yuck said, running out of
the door on his way to school.

"I said no smelly socks!" the Dragon
boomed. She was standing at the classroom
door, pinching her nose.

"But they're my favourites, Miss," Yuck told her.

"I'll have no smelly socks in my class!"

She let all the other children in, then slammed the door.

From the corridor Yuck pressed his nose against the glass.

He watched as the Dragon walked around the room seeing what everyone was writing. She prodded Little Eric with her umbrella.

Yuck pulled the blank piece of paper from his pocket, chewed his pencil and thought for a second, then sneaked off to the school kitchens.

He could smell fish. Mrs Dollop was
preparing the school lunch. When she
wasn't looking, Yuck tiptoed in and pinched
two fish fingers. He jammed one into each
sock. Then he stuffed in a handful of
cabbage and poured a bowlful of lumpy
custard and half a jug of cold gravy on top.

It dribbled down his ankles and leaked into his shoes, sloshing up and down as he ran back down the corridor and stood outside the Dragon's classroom.

Cheesy, fishy socks!

Yuck wiggled his toes until home time.

"What did you do today, Yuck?" Mum asked, when he got home that evening.

"We're writing poems," Yuck told her.

"I heard that you were sent out of class," Polly said.

Yuck buttered two slices of bread and took some more cheese from the fridge.

"I also heard that everyone else has nearly finished their poems and that you'll ALL be reading them out to the whole school at the end of the week."

"Megan the Mouth should keep her mouth shut," Yuck said.

"So what's your poem about, Yuck?" Mum asked.

"Or haven't you done it?" Polly said.

"It's a secret," Yuck told them.

He made himself a cheese sandwich,
grabbed a bottle of ketchup and went
upstairs to his bedroom.

"Please can no one disturb me."

Yuck pinned a sign on his door saying
POET AT WORK and wedged his chair
under the door handle so no one could
come in.

Opening his cheese sandwich, he peeled back the two slices of bread and sniffed.

"Mmmm… cheeeeeeese!"

He took his shoes and socks off, broke the cheese into little lumps and wedged them between his toes.

With one slice of buttered bread in each hand, he wiped the butter over his feet, then stuck the slices together again with ketchup.

There was a knock at his door.

Yuck put his goggles on and picked up the baseball bat…

"What are you doing in there?" Polly demanded.

"I'm writing my poem," Yuck said.

Polly rattled the door handle and pushed.

"Go away, Polly!"

Yuck spooned the soggy mess into his socks, slipped them back on and hopped into bed.

Everything squelched as he wiggled his toes.

That night, Yuck dreamed he was at
cheese school. The whole school was made
of cheese. The doors were made of cheese,
the desks were made of cheese and the
chairs were made of cheese. And when
the Dragon poked him, her umbrella turned
to cheese. Yuck ate it between two big slices
of bread.

When he woke up, his socks were smellier
than ever.

"Have you got clean socks on?" Mum
called as he ran out of the door.

"Yes Mum," Yuck said.

But when he got to school…

"No smelly socks in my classroom!" the Dragon boomed.

Yuck stood in the corridor.

He waited until everyone was at their desks and the Dragon was walking among them, poking them, then he sneaked off down the corridor, out into the playground.

He ran to the school pond and scooped out a handful of frogspawn and stinky pond water. He poured it into one sock. Then he scooped out a handful of green slime and fish poo and slipped it into the other.

A frog hopped out of the pond.

"Ribbit!"

Yuck ran back and stood outside the
Dragon's classroom, squelching in a
pondwater puddle until the end of the day.

"What's for dinner?" he asked when
he got home.

"Pizza," Mum replied.

"Rockits!" Yuck said, and he took an
extra slice up to his room.

Wedging his chair behind his bedroom
door, he set to work.

He took the slice of cheesy pizza and wiped it around his feet, getting the tomato sauce and cheese deep under his toenails.

There was a knock at the door.

"What's that smell?" Polly called. "I can smell something through the door."

"It must be your breath," Yuck said.

Just at that moment, a frog hopped out of one of his socks.

"Ribbit!"

"And what was that noise?" Polly asked.

"Go away, Polly!"

The frog flicked its long tongue and licked Yuck's cheesy toes, covering them with frog spit.

"Good boy," Yuck said.

He picked the frog up and put it on his desk.

He put his goggles on and picked up the baseball bat.

The frog croaked.

Yuck wiped a piece of ham sandwich
from the bat and gave it to the frog to eat.
"Don't worry, I'm not going to hurt you."

And as Yuck slipped his socks on and
hopped into bed, the frog hopped after him
and licked his toes while he slept.

That night, Yuck dreamed he was
paddling in the sea.

He dipped his toes in the water, and
all the fish jumped out, shouting,
"Phwoarrr! Cheesy!"

When he woke, his socks were slimier and smellier than ever.

That day, there was a note waiting for him on the classroom door.

NO SMELLY SOCKS!

Rockits! Yuck thought.

He sneaked off and, in the bushes by the school gate, found two slugs, some bird poo and some cat sick. Phwoarrr!

He dropped a slug into each sock, then wiped the bird poo and the cat sick over his toes.

When he got home, he went to the kitchen cupboard and fetched a pot of extra-hot mustard, an onion, some garlic and a bag of cheesy crisps. He took everything up to his room.

A little later, there was a knock at his bedroom door.

"What's going on in there?" Polly asked. "It smells very cheesy."

"I'm writing my poem," Yuck said.

"No you're not. And tomorrow you're

going to be in BIG TROUBLE when Mrs Wagon finds out."

"Go away, Polly!"

Yuck added a spoonful of extra-hot mustard to each sock, then put on his goggles, picked up his baseball bat and...

He crushed the onion, the garlic and the crisps into tiny pieces and sprinkled them over his toes.

He pulled his socks back on and hopped into bed.

Yuck wiggled his toes – everything felt nice and sweaty.

He heard a "Ribbit!" from under the duvet and felt a long wet tongue flick over his ankles.

"Good night," Yuck said to his frog.

That night, Yuck dreamed he was in a land where everything was stains and smells. He met cheesy people with garlic hats and farting dogs and crusty cats...

When Yuck woke up, he threw back his duvet and a cheesy cloud erupted from his socks. They were ready! The dirtiest, crustiest, smelliest socks in the whole wide world!

"Are you wearing clean socks today?"
Mum asked when she saw him.

"Yes, Mum!" Yuck replied, and he ran
out of the door.

On the way to school, Yuck passed two
dogs that were sniffing one another's
bottoms. When they saw him, they
ran over, sniffed his socks, barked and
ran away.

My socks smell worse than a dog's
bottom! he thought. This is going to be fun.

But when he arrived at school, the Dragon was waiting for him.

In her hand she was holding a pair of CLEAN socks!

"But, Miss!" Yuck said.

"Put these on!" she told him, and she dragged Yuck to assembly.

"I hope you've written your poem. We're all waiting to hear it."

Everyone was sitting on the floor.

The Dragon walked to the stage. Mr Reaper the headmaster was standing at the front. "Today, Mrs Wagon's class are going to read us their poems," he announced to the school.

"Who would like to go first?"

No one put their hand up.

"Come on – don't be shy!"
Little Eric hid behind Yuck.
"What's that smell?" Little Eric asked.

"Yuck!" the Dragon called. "Yuck will go first!"

Polly was sitting at the front with Juicy Lucy. She grinned as Yuck was made to walk through the crowd to the front of the room.

He stepped up onto the stage.

"I'm pleased to see you are wearing

clean socks today, Yuck," the Dragon
said, grinning.

Yuck looked down at the clean socks
on his feet, and walked to the centre of
the stage.

His hands were in his pockets, fumbling
for something.

He pulled out a piece of paper.

"My poem is called…"

The piece of paper was blank.

"What's that?" Polly whispered to Lucy.

"Yuck's poem."

"No, not that. Look!"

Yuck was wearing something red on
his hands.

He sniffed and smiled. "My poem is called… 'I Wandered Lonely as a Cheese'."

The Dragon looked at the Reaper. The Reaper's nose twitched.

Yuck sniffed his hands and smiled.

"I wandered lonely as a cheese,
To a land of smelly make-believe,
Where (as this pongy poem tells),
Everything was stains and smells."

"Why is he wearing gloves?" Lucy asked.

Polly squinted. "Those aren't gloves! Those are his smelly socks!"

Yuck was sniffing, making up his poem
from the different smells:

"Cheesy people and garlic hats,
Farting dogs and crispy cats,
Banana shoes and slugs for sweets,
Pond-water puddles and gravy streets."

Polly rushed to the front.
"He's wearing his smelly socks on
his hands!"
The Dragon looked at Yuck. "Yuck—!"

But as she opened her mouth to speak, a great cloud of cheesy gas wafted from Yuck's smelly socks and she swallowed it.

"Cabbage houses and pizza stairs,
Oily tables and greasy chairs,
Mouldy picnics and onion pies,
Fish-finger grass and frogspawn skies."

The children in the front row coughed. The Dragon leaned against the Reaper to steady herself. Her tongue was lolling out of her mouth. Her eyes were rolling.

"Uuurgh!" she screamed, breathing in the thick cheesy cloud as it billowed through the room.

"Ketchup cars and eggy trains,
Fish-poo boats and bird-poo planes,
Mustard ponds and custard lakes,
Frog-spit drinks and cat-sick cakes."

Slowly, the thick cheesy cloud drifted across the children. They felt dizzy. They began to sweat.

Polly sniffed.

"Get him off!" she cried, but when she opened her mouth, the cheesy gas went in.

Polly fainted.

"Evacuate the building!" the Reaper gasped.

"Keep going, Yuck!" Little Eric called out.

"Stains and smells were everywhere,
Noses sniffing cheesy air,
But much more smelly than all these things,
Were my smelly socks, so they made me KING!"

The cheesy cloud from Yuck's socks floated up to the ceiling, then all at once, water started pouring down.

Yuck's smelly socks had set off the sprinklers!

"Poetry's cancelled!" the Reaper called, dragging the Dragon out of the hall by her ankles.

The children coughed and cheered.

Yuck smiled and took a bow, and everyone crawled out of the room spluttering. All of them were soaking wet.

Then came the sound of a siren.

It was a fire engine, come to find the source of the poisonous gas.

Mum got quite a surprise when she heard the doorbell and opened the front door to see a fireman in a gas mask, holding Yuck's smelly socks in a plastic bag.

"I think these need washing, Madam," the fireman said. He handed the smelly socks to Mum.

Yuck stepped out from behind the fireman.

"Thanks for the ride, Mister," he said.
And he stepped inside.
Mum closed the door.
"YUCK!"
Then the doorbell rang again. This time it
was an ambulance man. Polly was standing

beside him, wrapped in a blanket. She was coughing and spluttering.

"They've evacuated the school because of a poisonous gas," the ambulance man said.

Polly stepped inside.

Mum closed the door.

"Yuck! These are going in the washing machine NOW!"

She was holding his socks, pinching her nose. "They're disgusting!"

Yuck followed Mum into the kitchen, took one last sniff and watched as Mum opened the door of the washing machine and threw his smelly socks inside.

But just as she was closing the door on the front of the machine...

"Wait a minute, Mum," Yuck said. "I've got some more."

"More!"

Yuck ran upstairs.

"I want every last pair!" Mum called up after him.

Yuck ran to his room and fetched all the clean socks from his sock drawer. He ran back into the kitchen with his arms full of socks and stuffed them all in the machine.

"You're disgusting, Yuck," Mum said. "From now on, it's clean socks EVERY day!" She closed the door of the washing

machine, picked up a box of SUPERSUDS
washing powder and poured some in the
top. Then she poured in some more – just
to make sure.

Cleans all known stains and smells, Yuck
read on the box.

We'll see about that, he thought.

He crossed his fingers.

When the SUPERSUDS were in, Mum
turned the machine on to FULL POWER.

Yuck, Mum and Polly stood in front of
the washing machine and watched. The
machine filled up with water and started
to whirl.

The SUPERSUDS foamed.
The machine made noises.
It growled.
It groaned.

Yuck's socks spun faster and faster.

The SUPERSUDS and his smelly socks were locked in battle.

Yuck could see lumps of cheese, pieces of fish finger and bits of cat sick spinning round and round.

The SUPERSUDS frothed. The water
started bubbling and boiling.

Yuck saw bird poo, frogspawn and pizza.
The machine was whining and gurgling.

"What's happening?" Polly asked.

"SUPERSUDS can clean anything,"
Mum said.

But at that moment there was a huge

clang – then a crunch. The machine
stopped.

Mum and Polly looked at each other.

The door of the washing machine
sprang open, belching a thick cloud
of cheesy gas.

"UUURRRGGGHHH!" Mum and
Polly cried.

Yuck reached in and pulled out his socks.
He took a big sniff and smiled.

"Rockits!"

Now all his socks were smelly!

"Nothing beats my smelly socks!"

Look out for more great adventures with

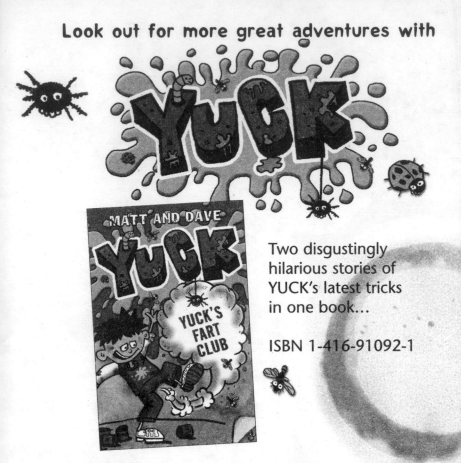

Two disgustingly
hilarious stories of
YUCK's latest tricks
in one book...

ISBN 1-416-91092-1

YUCK'S FART CLUB – Yuck has a brilliant idea for a club and
he's inviting all his friends! Who would have thought they
could make so many types of farts? But his sister, Polly, is
determined to find out what Yuck is up to – and she's in for
an explosive surprise!

YUCK'S SICK TRICK – Yuck does NOT want to go to school.
He's got a spelling test and he'll do absolutely anything to
get out of it. Even if it means showing the whole family how
revoltingly sick he can be...

Look out for more YUCK books coming soon
by visiting www.yuckweb.com